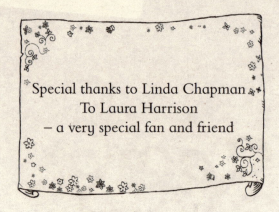

Special thanks to Linda Chapman
To Laura Harrison
– a very special fan and friend

ORCHARD BOOKS

First published in Great Britain in 2013 by Orchard Books
This edition published in 2017 by The Watts Publishing Group

3 5 7 9 10 8 6 4

A CIP catalogue record for this book is available from the British Library.

ISBN 978 1 40834 832 1

Printed in Great Britain by Clays Ltd, Elcograf S.p.A.

The paper and board used in this book are made from wood from responsible sources

Orchard Books
An imprint of Hachette Children's Group
Part of The Watts Publishing Group Limited
Carmelite House, 50 Victoria Embankment, London EC4Y 0DZ

An Hachette UK Company
www.hachette.co.uk
www.hachettechildrens.co.uk

Series created by Hothouse Fiction
www.hothousefiction.com

Fairytale
Forest

ROSIE BANKS

ORCHARD

This is the Secret Kingdom

Fairytale Forest

Contents

Books! Books! Books!

Summer Hammond ran her finger slowly along the spines of the books on the library shelf. There were so many books with so many stories in! She pushed her long blonde plaits back over her shoulders and felt happiness run through her as she tried to decide which book to pick. She loved reading and the library was one of her favourite places to go.

So when Ellie Macdonald, one of her best friends, had said she needed to come and find a book for her art project, Summer had been eager to come with her, and they'd dragged their other best friend, Jasmine Smith, along as well!

Ellie was looking through a big art book all about making puppets. "This book is just what I need for my school project," she said in a low voice so the librarian wouldn't tell them off for talking. "I'm going to sit down and make some notes."

Jasmine sat down next to her. "How long will you be?" she sighed.

"I'm not sure," Ellie replied.

"Why don't you come and choose a book while we wait?" Summer said to Jasmine.

But Jasmine shook her head. "No. I'll just sit here. I'm not really keen on reading."

Summer knew Jasmine much preferred singing and dancing and being active to reading quietly. But surely there was a book her friend would like? There had to be!

She started looking on the shelves. There! She spotted the perfect book. "Try this one!" She took it off the shelf and carried it over.

Jasmine read the title. *"Pandora Parks: Pop Star!"* The girl on the cover looked quite like her, with long dark hair and brown eyes. She was holding a microphone and was dressed in a red catsuit. Jasmine turned it over to read the description on the back cover.

"Actually, this book does look quite good," she admitted.

"Try reading it," Summer encouraged her. "There's a whole series of books about Pandora. She's a pop star in one book, an actress in another, and then a model, and she has loads of adventures. I bet you'll like them and..." Summer grinned as she realised that Jasmine was already turning over the first page. Summer smiled to herself and then went back to the shelf. Now, which book was she going to read?

She pulled out several books before she decided on an animal rescue story. She sat down with the others and began reading.

After about half an hour, Ellie shut her notebook. "Okay, I've got all the notes I need for my school project. Now I just need to go home and actually make the puppet!" She stood up and put the book back on the shelf.

Summer stretched and got to her feet too. She looked over to where Jasmine still had her head buried in *Pandora Parks: Pop Star!* "Jasmine, we're going back to Ellie's house."

Jasmine blinked. "But I'm at a really exciting bit. I can't stop reading now!"

Summer chuckled. "So, maybe you're keen on reading *some* books then?"

"Definitely this one. It's amazing!"
Jasmine grinned. "I'll have to borrow
it from the library so I can finish it.
Pandora has so many adventures!"

Ellie overheard. "Like us!"

The three friends grinned at each other.
They shared a very special secret. At
their school jumble sale they had found
an old carved wooden box. It had turned
out to be a magic box made by King
Merry, who ruled an enchanted land
called the Secret Kingdom. Whenever
the people of the Secret Kingdom needed
the girls' help, their pixie friend Trixibelle
would send them a message in the box,
then whisk them away to the wonderful
land.

"Where's the Magic Box now?"
whispered Jasmine.

"Here," said Ellie, putting her bag on the table and patting it.

"I wonder when we'll get another message from the Secret Kingdom?" Summer said.

Ellie opened the top of her bag and brought the Magic Box out. Its wooden sides were carved with magical creatures and its lid was studded with six green gems. "Oh, I wish it would glow!" she said longingly.

A bright light flashed across the mirrored lid of the box.

"It worked!" Ellie exclaimed in astonishment.

Jasmine looked hopefully at the box. "I wish I had a million pounds!"

"Ssh!" the librarian scolded from her desk.

"Come on!" said Ellie, pushing the box back into her bag. Her eyes sparkled with excitement. "The Secret Kingdom needs us! We'd better find somewhere more private where we can look at the box properly and see if it has a message for us."

"Follow me!" Heart pounding, Summer led the way out of the children's section and down the aisles. Another adventure was starting! "I wonder where in the Secret Kingdom we'll have to go this time!" she whispered.

"And what ingredient we'll be trying to find!" said Jasmine.

The Secret Kingdom was in real trouble. King Merry's sister, evil Queen Malice, had given him a cake with a potion inside. He was now slowly turning into a horrible creature called a stink toad. Queen Malice planned to take over the kingdom when the transformation was complete. The only way to stop the curse was to give King Merry a magical counter-potion, but to make it they needed six very rare ingredients. So far, they had collected bubblebee honeycomb, silverspun sugar,

dream dust and some healing water from
Clearsplash Waterfall. There were just
two ingredients left to get!

They reached the far corner of the
library, which was full of volumes of
dusty old leather-bound journals. "We
should be safe here," Summer whispered.
"No one ever comes down this aisle."

The girls kneeled down and took out
the Magic Box from Ellie's bag. Its
mirrored lid was still shining brightly
with a silver light. The girls watched as
curly letters appeared and formed into
words. Jasmine read them out:

"Ellie, Summer, Jasmine, please,
Look for somewhere that has trees.
Find the place where tales all grow.
That is where you have to go!"

As she finished speaking, sparkles
rippled across the surface of the box
and the lid magically sprang open. Inside
the box there were six compartments,
each containing a different magic object.
One of them was a beautiful map of
the Secret Kingdom, which now floated
out and opened itself up in front of the
girls' eyes.

Summer gazed down in delight at the beautiful crescent-shaped island through the magic map.

"Look, there are the dream dragons!" whispered Ellie, pointing to a peaceful valley where the beautiful creatures snoozed underneath pink-and-white cherry blossom trees.

"And Lily Pad Lake!" said Jasmine, pointing to the place where they'd had their last adventure. Blue-skinned water nymphs were splashing in the clear water with their giant water-snail pets.

"Where do we have to go this time?" Summer wondered, her eyes scanning the map. "It says, *somewhere where tales grow…*"

Ellie frowned. "Maybe it means a jungle? You get monkeys in a jungle, and they have tails."

"It's not that sort of tail," said Summer. "It's spelled T – A – L – E – S in the riddle. You know, like fairy tales."

"Maybe it's a library!" suggested Jasmine. "Let's see if we can find one." They all looked carefully at the map, but they couldn't see a library anywhere.

Ellie re-read the clue. "Wait a second! It doesn't just say about tales, it also says we have to find a place which has trees."

"What about here?" said Summer, pointing to a woodland where tall trees were growing with green grass and cheerful red-and-white toadstools all around them. She read the label out and gasped. "Fairytale Forest! That's got to be it!"

"I bet you're right!" said Jasmine.

"Definitely." Ellie peered closer. "But the trees look strange."

Summer saw what she meant. The trees seemed to have odd rectangular leaves. "I'm sure Trixi will know what they are." She smiled. "Let's call her!"

The girls all put their hands on the green gems and looked at one another.

"The answer to the riddle is Fairytale Forest!" they chorused.

Fairytale Forest

There was a bright pink flash. The map flew back inside the box and the girls heard a tiny gasp up above their heads. They all looked up.

"Trixi!" Jasmine gasped.

Their pixie friend was perched on her floating leaf on top of the bookshelf. She was looking round in astonishment, her big blue eyes wide.

"Look at all these books!" she cried.

"Sssh!" said Summer hastily, not wanting the librarian to come over. She wasn't quite sure how they would explain Trixi to her!

Trixi flew her leaf into the air and floated down to them. She was wearing a knee-length emerald-green dress decorated with silver swirls and she had a silver headband holding back her messy golden hair. "Where are we?" she asked.

"In Honeyvale Library," whispered Ellie. "But we have to be quiet or the librarian will hear."

"Sorry!" Trixi whispered back. She kissed each of them on the nose. "It's lovely to see you all."

"And you," said Summer. "We got your message. Is the next ingredient in Fairytale Forest?"

Trixi clapped her tiny hands together. "Yes! Aunt Maybelle has just discovered that the fifth ingredient we need for the counter-potion is a book bud. And the only place to find one is in Fairytale Forest."

"What's a book bud?" Jasmine asked curiously.

Trixi blinked. "You don't know what a book bud is?" She looked at them as they all shook their heads. "But you have books here in your world," she said, gesturing at the shelves. "So you must have book buds, or else how do they grow?"

The three girls exchanged confused looks. "*Grow?*" Ellie echoed. "Books don't grow."

"Don't grow?" Trixi stared. "Whatever do you mean? Of course they grow!"

"No. In our world, books are *made*, not grown," explained Summer.

"What happens in the Secret Kingdom, Trixi?" asked Jasmine curiously.

Trixi smiled. "Wait and see! Are you ready to go to Fairytale Forest?"

"Oh yes!" the three friends cried.

Trixi flew a loop-the-loop on her leaf. "Then let's go! King Merry is getting more toad-like every day. There's not a second to lose!" The girls grabbed one another's hands as Trixi tapped her magical pixie ring and called out in her musical voice:

"Good friends fly to break the curse
Before King Merry gets much worse!"

Sparkling light swirled around them,
whisking the girls away. They held
on tightly to one another as they spun
about. As they were set down they heard
the sound of birds singing and felt soft
grass beneath their feet.

The sparkling cloud cleared and they saw that they were standing in the middle of an enormous wood with tall trees all around them. Sunlight shone down through the tree branches, sending dappled light onto the lush grass. Beautiful flowers were dotted about along with knee-height red-and-white toadstools. Bluebirds swooped through the air and rabbits peered out

shyly from behind tree trunks, their
noses twitching and their ears flickering.
Large pale-yellow seed pods twirled
down through the air and landed in the
girls' hair. Jasmine jumped into the air
and caught one. "We have these in our
world, but they're much smaller!" she
said.

As Summer reached up to brush a
pod away she felt her tiara and smiled.
Whenever the girls arrived in the Secret
Kingdom, special tiaras would appear
on their heads so that everyone who met
them would know they were the human
girls from the Other Realm who had
come to help them.

"So, what do you think of Fairytale
Forest?" said Trixi excitedly as she darted
about through the sunny glade on her
little leaf. "This is where all our books
grow! Look!" She pointed upwards.

The girls glanced into the branches of
the trees and gasped. Hundreds of books
were growing up there, attached to the
branches like leaves!

"Oh, wow!" exclaimed Jasmine.
"Books really *do* grow on trees in the

Secret Kingdom!"

"Of course they do!" Trixi smiled.

It really was the most amazing sight.
The pages of the books
fluttered in the
breeze. "What are
those little green
things?" said
Ellie, pointing to
some little green
balls on some of
the branches.

"They're book
buds," answered
Trixi. "Each of them
will bloom into a book when they're
ready. The book brownies who live in
the forest look after the trees and pick the
books."

Summer longed to climb a tree and look at the books hanging there. "Oh, I wish books grew on trees in our world!" she sighed longingly. "It would be amazing!"

Ellie grinned. "You'd build a tree house and never come down!"

"Hello, there," a curious voice said. They all spun round and saw a small creature coming towards them. "May I help you?"

"It's a book brownie!" exclaimed Trixi.

The book brownie looked a bit like one of the gnomes some people had in their gardens in Honeyvale Village. He was about half the height of the girls and had a wrinkled face and long beard. His nut-brown eyes twinkled as he looked at them. "So what can I do for you? I…"

He saw their tiaras and broke off. "Oh,
my goodness gracious! You must be the
three human girls from the Other Realm
– I've always wanted to meet you!"

Summer smiled. "Hello. I'm Summer.
This is Ellie and Jasmine and this is Trixi,
King Merry's royal pixie."

"Well, I'm delighted to meet you all! Thoroughly delighted," said the book brownie, beaming. "I'm Dickon. I live and work here in Fairytale Forest with all my friends and family. So, have you come here to find a book, my dears?"

"Actually we're here because we're trying to help King Merry again," Jasmine replied. She and the others quickly explained what had been happening.

"We really need a book bud for the counter-potion," said Summer. "If we can get one then we'll only have one ingredient left to find."

"King Merry has to drink the counter-potion by midnight on the day of the Summer Ball," added Ellie. "Otherwise it will be too late and he'll be stuck as a

stink toad forever. Please will you
help us?"

"Of course I will!" said the book
brownie. "In fact, you've arrived at
the perfect time. The book buds are
all blooming into books, but there are
still a few left. Come through and meet
everyone and we'll get you a book bud
from one of the trees."

Exchanging delighted looks, the girls
followed Dickon to the next clearing. As
they came through the trees they looked
around in wonder. There were ladders
leaning against the gnarled trunks and
lots of book brownies scurrying up and
down them with rectangular wicker
baskets in their hands. The brownies
were gently picking the books off the
branches and placing them inside the

baskets side by side, as if they were on a bookshelf. When their baskets were full they brought them down and stacked the books in piles on a wooden cart in the clearing that was lined with shelves. The girls stared round, open-mouthed.

"What happens to all the books?" asked Summer.

"We put one copy of every book that is ever grown into the Fairytale Forest

Library, and the other copies we send around the kingdom so everyone can enjoy them," Dickon explained. "Let's find you a book bud," he added, rubbing his hands together. "There are plenty over here." He led them to a slender tree with lots of green buds on its branches. As they looked at it, one of the buds slowly started to unfurl.

"What's happening to it?" Ellie asked in wonder.

"It's blooming into a book!" said Dickon happily. "Watch closely!"

They all stared as the green petals on the outside of the bud peeled back, revealing a plain green book in the centre of the bud.

But it didn't stay plain for long. In front
of the girls' eyes, beautiful silver words
started forming on the cover.

"*The Three Unicorns Gruff*," Summer
read out as a picture formed on the cover
too. Then the book opened itself up and
the pages began turning over. The girls
saw words and colourful illustrations
appearing on them as they flipped by.
On the last page, the words "The End"
appeared and the book shut with a snap.

"That's it! The book is ready to be
picked," Dickon declared.

"That is the most amazing thing I have
ever seen!" breathed Jasmine.

"Now, let's get you a book bud before
they all bloom." Dickon turned to the
other brownies. "Weatherstaff, would
you fetch a ladder, please, so we can

help the human girls and Trixi?"

A book brownie with a cheerful smile, long grey beard, bushy moustache and round glasses brought

a ladder over. "Of course I'll get you a book bud," he said. "We'd do anything to help King Merry."

"Thank you!" said Summer. "We really need to get one to Aunt Maybelle as soon as possible before Queen Malice tries to stop us!"

Just then there was a booming, cackling laugh. "Ha! Too late!"

They all jumped in alarm. Summer's heart leaped into her throat as the tall figure of Queen Malice stalked through the trees towards them, a white mist rolling around her feet. Her skirt swept through the forest and her bony fingers were clutching her spiky black staff. "So, you are trying to get a book bud, are you?" she demanded.

"Yes!" said Jasmine bravely, stepping in front of Dickon. "And you can't stop us!"

"Oh, I think I can!" snapped the queen, her eyes glittering wickedly.

"How?" said Ellie. "There are loads of book buds!"

"Not for much longer!" Queen Malice raised her staff and shrieked with laughter. "Not when I make them wither and die!"

Queen Malice's Evil Plan

Lightning crackled from the end of Queen Malice's black staff.

"No!" gasped the girls.

"Queen Malice, please don't!" pleaded Dickon.

The other brownies had seen what was happening and were scrambling down the trees and running over, all shouting and protesting. Queen Malice just laughed. "Who needs books anyway?

I hate them all! Silly stories about pixies, fairies, brownies and elves all living happily ever after. Pah! Ridiculous!"

"Please, Queen Malice, please don't destroy the books!" begged Trixi, flying towards the queen.

"Out of my way, stupid pixie!" cried Queen Malice, lifting her other hand and knocking Trixi flying. She called out a spell:

"Reading is ruined when books and buds die. Dry up, wither, fall down from on high!"

She shook her staff and white lightning flashed through the wood. It seemed

to touch every tree and every branch.
Queen Malice shrieked in delight as
all around them the pages of the books
started crumpling and curling, turning
red and gold.

"Oh, no!" gasped Summer. "It's like the
leaves in our world falling off the trees in
the autumn!"

As the books
dried up the
pages fell
out from
the covers
and
floated
down to
the ground,
raining on the
heads of the girls and the brownies.

"Stop it!" shouted Jasmine as the book buds on the branches turned brown and scrunched up into tiny balls.

"Oh, no!" Summer cried as the book buds began dropping off the branches and falling onto the grass. Soon all that was left were little dried-up husks.

Ellie rushed over and picked one up. It crumbled to dust in her hand.

Summer gave a sob. She couldn't bear it. Ellie put her arm round her friend's shoulders while Jasmine helped Trixi up from under the pile of crunchy brown book pages that had covered her.

"Storm Sprites!" Queen Malice shrieked. Four familiar creatures with bat-like wings and pointed faces flew out of the sky and perched on the now-empty branches of the trees.

"Stay here and make sure these meddling girls don't find a book bud. Not that they are likely to." Queen Malice gave another cackle. "Because there aren't any left!" She clapped her hands gleefully and disappeared in a crash of thunder.

The book brownies all looked horrified, and many of them were in tears. "All our lovely books!" exclaimed Weatherstaff. "Now there won't be any new stories for anyone!"

"Oh, I'm so, so sorry," cried Trixi in dismay. "Queen Malice is so awful!"

"All the books are ruined," said Summer, aghast.

"And now there's no book bud for King Merry's potion," said Jasmine.

"HA! King Merry's going to turn into a stink toad!" jeered one of the Storm Sprites. "And our queen will rule the land!" The other Storm Sprites laughed and dived down, landing in the piles of fallen pages with shrieks of glee. They started throwing them up into the air, crowing in delight.

"No more books for the brownies to pick," taunted another sprite. "Just dried-up pages on the floor!"

"Books are stupid anyway," said a third, throwing more pages into the air.

Dickon shook his fist at them. "Go away, you miserable things."

"Can't make us!" laughed the Storm Sprites, flapping their bat-like wings. "It's a free forest!"

Summer turned to Dickon. "Is there anything we can do to make the books grow again?"

"Stupid books! Stupid brownies!" cackled the sprites.

"There must be something we can do," said Jasmine.

The sprites shrieked and laughed as they jumped up and down.

"I can't hear myself think," said Ellie above the noise of the jeering. "Can we go somewhere quiet to talk? Maybe we can help you think of something to do."

"Let's go to the Fairytale Forest Library," suggested Dickon. "It's just through those trees over there."

With the sprites flapping behind them and calling out insults, the brownies and the girls hurried through the forest until they reached the most enormous oak tree. It was the tallest tree the girls had ever seen, stretching above them as high as a skyscraper. At the base of it there was a small red door, and round windows had been carved out of its gnarled trunk all the way up to the top.

"Welcome to the library," said Dickon, unlocking the door with a golden key.

The girls had
to duck to get
in through
the doorway
but once they
were inside
they found
they could
straighten up.
They gasped.
They were
standing
inside the
hollowed-
out tree in
a huge room that
went all the way up inside the trunk.
The walls were lined with bookshelves
and sunshine streamed in through the

round windows. A quiet, calm feeling
hung in the air.

"What
an amazing
library!"
breathed
Summer.

A golden
staircase
spiralled all the
way to the top
of the tree, with
little galleries
where people
could step off
and get a book.
At the bottom of
the staircase there were comfy sofas and
beanbags scattered over the floor.

"Look at all the books in here!" said Jasmine, her eyes wide.

"There's a copy of every book that's ever grown here in the Secret Kingdom," said Dickon proudly. He locked the door after them, keeping the sprites out. The sprites flew up and pressed their pointed long noses against the windows, sticking out their tongues and pulling horrible faces. The girls ignored them.

"It's wonderful!" said Summer, looking round at the sheer number of books lining the shelves. She went over to the nearest shelf and read the titles: *Cinderpixie; The Elf and the Pea; Little Red Riding Fairy...*

Summer grinned.

Jasmine joined her and looked at the titles too. "Do you have any books

about pop stars or adventures?" she asked
Dickon.

Dickon looked surprised. "What's
a pop star? All the stories that grow
in the Secret Kingdom have the same
characters – pixies, fairies, elves..."

"This is my favourite," said
Weatherstaff, pulling out one called
*Snow White Unicorn and the Seven
Brownies* and showing it to the girls.

"So you don't have *Pandora Parks:
Pop Star*?" Jasmine asked.

Dickon shook his head. "No. I have
to say I've never heard of that particular
fairy tale."

"It's not a fairy tale," said Jasmine.

Dickon looked surprised. "Not a fairy
tale?"

"Yes. We have fairy tales – ones a

bit like yours — but we also have lots of other books too," Summer explained. "Exciting ones, funny ones, scary ones, sad ones. All sorts."

"Goodness gracious," said Dickon in surprise, looking at Weatherstaff. "I've never heard anything like it."

Weatherstaff sighed. "There won't be *any* new books now for ages in the Secret Kingdom, fairy tales or not." He and all the other brownies sat down heavily on the sofas and beanbags.

"What are we going to do?" said one of them.

"Can't we plant some more trees?" Jasmine suggested hopefully.

"We could. We do have more seeds," said Dickon. Going to a wooden cabinet, he opened a drawer and took out a large green striped seed. "This is what they look like."

"We could help you plant them – I'm good at helping my granddad in the garden," Ellie offered.

"I'm afraid it isn't a quick job. You see, before a book tree seed can be planted you have to tell it a story so it knows what books to grow," Dickon replied. He sat down. "Why don't we show you? Join in, please do!" he urged the girls. "We need to sit in a circle – the magic always seems to work best if we make a circle." The girls, Trixi and the brownies made a circle around Dickon. He held the seed carefully in his hands and began to tell it a story.

"Once upon a time, there was a young pixie called Emeraldlocks. She had the most beautiful green hair anyone had ever seen. One day she went into the woods on her own and came across a little cottage where three dragons lived: a baby dragon, a mother dragon and a father dragon."

Jasmine nudged Ellie. "I think I know what happens in this story!" she whispered with a grin.

They listened as Dickon told a Secret Kingdom version of *Goldilocks and the Three Bears*. "And after that, Emeraldlocks went to visit the three dragons whenever she liked," Dickon finished at last. "The end!" As he spoke the last two words the seed started

to glow with a golden light. It shone and sparkled in Dickon's hand.

The girls gasped.

"It has been told its story!" said Dickon happily. "And now it's ready to be planted. If we look after it well it will grow into a book tree. Here we are, Weatherstaff."

He handed the seed to Weatherstaff, who put it carefully into his pocket.

"How long will it be before it grows book buds?" Jasmine asked eagerly.

"Five years," Dickon replied.

The girls looked at each other in dismay. "But we can't wait five years for the book bud for King Merry's potion!" exclaimed Ellie.

Trixi shook her head. "The king needs to drink the counter-potion before the

Summer Ball, and that's in a few weeks' time."

"What about the trees already in the wood?" asked Jasmine. "They haven't got books on them any more but they're fully grown. How long will it take them to grow new book buds?"

Dickon rubbed his beard. "It's usually between one and six months. Some trees grow book buds quickly and some grow them slowly. We've never been able to work out quite why one tree is different from another."

The other brownies shook their heads.

"Isn't there anything we can do to make the book buds grow faster?" said Summer.

"I'm afraid not." Dickon sighed heavily. "Oh dear, poor King Merry. You're not going to be able to get a book bud in time to make the counter-potion."

"We can't give up!" said Jasmine, thinking as hard as she could. Ellie and Summer racked their brains too.

"Wait a minute! I've had an idea!" Trixi cried suddenly, swooping up into the air on her leaf. "Why don't I try casting a growing spell? Pixie magic can make things happen super fast, so maybe I can make the book buds grow really quickly."

"Oh, Trixi, that would be brilliant!" Summer said in delight.

Trixi glanced at the windows where the sprites were leering in at them. "The sprites are bound to try and stop me."

Jasmine pushed her dark hair back behind her ears. "So what if they do?

We'll protect you. I'm not frightened of them!"

Ellie jumped to her feet. "Neither am I!"

Summer took a deep breath. "If there's any way we can grow a book bud, we will!"

Meddling Sprites

As the girls, Trixi and the brownies left the library, the Storm Sprites cackled and shouted nasty things at them. "You can't stop Queen Malice!" one yelled. "King Merry is going to be a stink toad forever!"

Trixi ignored them and pointed at the tree they were perched on. "Right, here goes," she said, holding up her ring and looking at the girls.

"What's she doing?" shrieked the sprites. "What's that pixie doing with her silly ring?"

Trixi chanted a spell:

"Pixie magic, make books grow.
Let it happen fast, not slow!"

A cloud of pink sparkles flew from her ring and fell on the tree's roots. Instantly the tree shot up to twice its old size, twenty book buds appeared and they all burst open, blooming into books in seconds.

The Storm Sprites shrieked in surprise, flapping out of the way of the growing leaves just in time.

"It worked!" Dickon exclaimed.

"But there aren't any buds left," Ellie

pointed out in disappointment. "The
books have bloomed straight away. The
magic made them grow *too* fast!"

"At least we have some more books," said Weatherstaff. He grabbed a ladder and climbed up to pick the books, but as he took hold of the first one and looked through it, the happiness left his eyes. "Oh," he said. He picked another one, looked inside and shook his head.

"What is it?" asked Jasmine.

Weatherstaff climbed down and showed them all the books. Summer skimmed the first pages. Instantly she saw what was wrong. "The words are all jumbled up!"

"The story in the book grew so fast it's all mixed up and in the wrong order," said Dickon. "These books are useless. Oh dear."

Trixi's face creased in disappointment as the Storm Sprites hooted with laughter. "Ha! You couldn't do it!"

Trixi landed on Jasmine's shoulder, her floating leaf drooping dejectedly.

"Never mind." Jasmine comforted the little pixie. "We're not going to give up. There must be something else we can do to make the book buds grow fast, but just not *that* fast."

"My granddad says he gets more flowers in his garden if his plants are kept warm and have food and water," Ellie said thoughtfully. "Maybe it would help if we watered and fed the trees and kept them warm. That might make the book buds grow again."

"It's certainly worth a try," agreed Dickon. He and Weatherstaff went over to talk to the watching brownies. A few minutes later they reappeared with some blankets, a long hosepipe and two wheelbarrows filled with crumbly brown fertiliser.

"Let's water the trees!" said Summer eagerly. The girls took the hosepipe and pointed the nozzles at the tree roots.

The brownies signalled through the trees for the water to be turned on. Overhead, the sprites flew together and whispered to one another in the empty branches of the trees. "I think they're up to something," Jasmine said grimly.

She was right. As soon as the water was turned on the sprites flew down. They swooped around, punching holes in the hosepipe with their spiky fingers. The water splurted out of the holes, spraying Summer, Jasmine, Ellie and the brownies.

"Turn the hose off!" Dickon shouted to

the other brownies, as he ducked under a
bush to avoid the spray.

The sprites flew upwards, cackling.
"Look how wet they are!" they cried.

"What a bunch of drips!" one laughed.

"They're not going to get any book
buds!" another gloated.

Jasmine squeezed the water out of her hair and looked anxiously at the trees. "I wonder if the water's helped at all?"

They all stared at the trees but they still looked exactly the same. There were no book buds on the bare branches.

Summer turned to the others. "The water doesn't seem to have done anything."

"Maybe we could try food and warmth?" Jasmine suggested.

The girls fetched the blankets and started wrapping them around the tree trunks, and then they went to the wheelbarrows. Each of them had a spade on top. The girls took the spades and started putting fertiliser onto the roots of the nearest tree but as they did, the sprites dived down with a series of whoops. First they tore the blankets away from the tree trunks and tossed them through the air. Then they flew to the wheelbarrows and started throwing handfuls of fertiliser at the girls.

"Oh, this is impossible!" cried Summer, dodging as a sprite tried to drop a handful on her head.

"Yuck!" exclaimed Ellie, shaking it out of her red curls.

"Stop it!" Jasmine said furiously to the sprites.

"No way!" one cackled, throwing a blanket right at her. "This is fun!"

Jasmine pulled the blanket off her head crossly.

"Come on, Jasmine, just ignore those silly sprites." Ellie led her over to a tree some way off.

"What are we going to do?" Summer sighed as the three of them sat down underneath the tree with Dickon, Weatherstaff and Trixi. "Even if we can somehow get the sprites to leave us alone, I think it's going to take too long for the book buds to grow."

Ellie sighed. "You're probably right. Trixi's magic worked too fast, but my idea is just too slow."

"We need another plan!" declared Jasmine. "Pandora Parks always comes up with lots of plans when she is in trouble. In the story I was reading at the library she was kidnapped and locked in a room. It looked like there was no way of escaping because her kidnappers didn't even open the door to feed her. They just pushed the food through a hatch."

"I've never heard a story like that!" Dickon said, blinking in surprise. "It sounds very exciting! Kidnappers! Having to escape from a locked room! I'd really like to read something like that."

Weatherstaff nodded eagerly. "It's not like any of the stories we have in our books here. What happens in it?"

"Well, Pandora pretends to be ill and when the kidnapper comes in to see if she's all right, she knocks him over and runs up the stairs and then escapes by hiding in a huge chest that's full of stage costumes. It's brilliant!" Jasmine said. "And I'm only halfway through!"

Summer had leaned back against the tree trunk, staring upwards at the branches and imagining the story in her head. As Jasmine was talking she was sure she saw a flash of green appear on the underneath of one of the branches above her head. "What's that?" she said, jumping to her feet to investigate. Just a bit higher than her head she found a tiny green leaf. "Look!" she gasped, pointing up at it.

The others scrambled to their feet too. "It appeared while you were telling the story, Jasmine!" Summer said excitedly.

"Goodness!" said Dickon. "How very surprising. I wonder why it grew like that."

An idea popped into Summer's head. "I think I know!" Her eyes shone. "You told us that the book tree seeds are different from normal seeds. Well, maybe book trees are different to normal trees. They don't need water and food to grow book buds more quickly – and they don't need pixie magic. They need something else!"

"What?" demanded Jasmine and Ellie.

Summer beamed. "Stories, of course!"

Story Magic

Summer explained her idea. "I think it's like the seeds needing stories before they can grow into book trees. Maybe stories also help the book trees in Fairytale Forest to bloom. Why don't we try telling a story to this tree and see if a book bud grows?"

"Excellent idea!" exclaimed Dickon, clapping his hands together. "I'd never have thought of that! Can we tell it an exciting story, like the one Jasmine was telling us?"

Weatherstaff nodded eagerly.

"Of course we can!" Summer said.

Ellie remembered something. "Maybe it will help if we sit in a circle. You said that always helps when you tell stories to the seeds."

Dicken nodded. "Let's try."

"Right, here goes," said Summer as they all sat in a circle around the bottom of the tree trunk.

"What are you doing?" The Storm Sprites flapped over to watch them.

"We're just going to tell each other a story," Summer said innocently.

The sprites looked at her suspiciously.
"A story? Why?"

"Well, you see, we've realised that you're just far too clever for us," Jasmine said, winking at Summer and Ellie. "We can see we'll never be able to beat you and get a book bud to grow, so we thought we might tell each other a story."

"To cheer ourselves up," Ellie put in, nodding hard.

The sprites looked very pleased with themselves. "We told you you would never beat us," crowed the leader.

"So you can go away now," Trixi said.

The Storm Sprites immediately looked wary again. "We're not leaving. You might get up to something."

The leader flapped over to the next tree and perched in the branches. "We'll watch you from here as you tell your

boring old story." The others followed
him, nodding. They sat there like giant
bats.

Summer looked round at the others.
"Right, I'll start." She thought for a
moment. She loved writing and making
up stories. She closed her eyes and
imagined…"Once upon a time there was
a girl called Pippa. She really loved wild
animals and one day her parents took
her to China. Pippa was really excited
because that was where the red pandas
lived. She had always wanted to see a
red panda and, um…"

Summer paused. What should happen
next? She glanced at Ellie and Jasmine.
Maybe they'd know.

"She'd also always wanted to paint
a red panda," Ellie said. "Pippa loved

painting, you see, and she was planning to enter a competition she'd seen in an art magazine. She had to do a painting of an animal and she thought it would be really cool to paint a red panda."

Summer gave Ellie a thumbs-up. "So, anyway, when she got to China she went into the forest to try and find a red panda," she continued. The green leaf hadn't got any bigger. "The forest was made of bamboo and she could hear all sorts of strange creatures and birds there. When she was wandering through the trees, she heard a whimpering cry and realised…"

"What?" said Dickon and Weatherstaff, excitedly.

"Oh, tell us! Tell us!" gasped Trixi, jumping up and down on her leaf.

Even the Storm Sprites were leaning
forward expectantly, with their eyes fixed
on Summer! "Go on!" they urged her,
not shrieking or jeering for once.

"Well, Pippa realised that there was a red panda in the bushes – in fact, not just one, but *four* red pandas! It was a mum and her cubs but the mum had got her paw caught in a trap! And then...and then…"

"Pippa gently freed the panda," Ellie took up the story again, "thinking all the time about how she would draw her rich red fur and bright dark eyes…"

"And I know what happened next! She'd just freed him when there were some shouts and along came a man!" gasped Jasmine. "He was a dangerous animal poacher and he grabbed Pippa and captured her! He took her to a house nearby and threw her in the cellar. She had no food or water and no way of getting out until suddenly she thought of a plan…"

Just then Summer spotted the green leaf growing bigger. She stifled her squeak of delight. "Go on, Jasmine!" she gasped.

"Pippa pretended to be ill," Jasmine continued. "And when the poacher came in she karate-chopped him and raced up the stairs and escaped outside. But then she was lost in the forest! Lost and alone!"

"Only she wasn't alone!" said Summer. "Because the red panda was there. It came bounding out of the bamboo with its cute cubs!"

"And it led Pippa safely home!" finished Ellie. Glancing up, she saw lots of green buds suddenly bursting out on all the branches. "It's worked!" She clapped her hands over her mouth and looked round at the Storm Sprites.

To her astonishment they were all still listening so raptly to the story that they hadn't even noticed the green buds on the branch above them.

"Is that what the girl said in the story?" one of the sprites demanded.

"Um…yes! She cheered and said: 'It worked!'" Ellie gabbled wildly, seeing everyone's curious looks. "'My plan worked! I got away from the poacher!'" Ellie's mind raced. The sprites mustn't see the book buds. "But, um…then before she got home something else really exciting happened," she went on quickly.

"What?" demanded all the sprites.

Ellie stood up and pretended to stretch. "You know, I think I'll tell the rest of it in the library," she said as casually as she could. She saw Summer and Jasmine's surprised looks. "If you look *up*, I'm sure you'll see some rain clouds coming," she said, raising her eyebrows and giving them both a meaningful stare.

Summer and Jasmine glanced upwards and saw the book buds on the tree branches. They both caught their breath in excitement. The storytelling had worked!

"I can't see any clouds," said one of the sprites, looking at the sky.

"I'm really sure I just saw one go by," Ellie said hastily.

"Me too. Let's tell the rest in the library," said Summer.

"Last one there is a stink toad!" said Jasmine, setting off at a run. Summer raced after her.

"Hey! Wait for us!" shrieked the sprites, flapping after them.

"I must hear the end of this story!" cried Dickon, hurrying towards the library as well. "I've never heard anything like it before and I really want to know what happens!"

"Me too!" said Weatherstaff.

"Trixi!" Ellie hissed, holding back.

"What, Ellie?" Trixi said impatiently, pausing her leaf in mid-air. "I want to hear what Pippa does next!"

"Look up!"

Trixi glanced up and saw the book buds. "Book buds!" she exclaimed. "Oh, Ellie!" She spun round. "There are hundreds of book buds on the tree!"

Happily Ever After

Ellie and Trixi stared up at the tiny green buds that were dotted over the branches of the huge story tree.

"I can't believe we found a way to make the book buds grow!" Trixi breathed.

"Can you fly up there and get one?" Ellie asked. "If you take it to Aunt Maybelle, we'll distract the Storm Sprites."

"Okay!" Trixi smiled. "But you will tell me how the story ends afterwards, won't you?" she added anxiously.

Ellie smiled. "Of course!"

Leaving Trixi to get a book bud, she raced after the others. They all were all just going inside with Weatherstaff and Dickon. The Storm Sprites flapped in and perched on the golden staircase while Summer sat down and carried on telling the story. "So, just as they were about to get to the house where Pippa was staying, she heard a shout and the poacher jumped out at her," she went on.

"He was about to throw a net over her," Ellie said, "but just then the red panda bit him on the bottom! He dropped the net and Pippa grabbed it and threw it over him. She had caught the poacher!"

"Pippa's parents were really pleased to see her," added Summer. "And the poacher was taken away by the police."

"And Pippa painted a brilliant picture of the red pandas and won the competition," said Ellie.

"Her prize was a trip to Mexico where she had even more adventures and became a film star!" Jasmine finished.

The girls looked at each other. "The end!" they declared triumphantly.

The sprites clapped. "That was a very exciting story!" said one.

"Maybe stories aren't stupid after all," another one admitted.

"I want to read some books," said a third, flying up to look through the books on the shelves.

"It really was a most incredible tale," Dickon said to the girls, his nut-brown eyes shining. "So much happened in it. I truly never realised stories could be like that." He turned to Weatherstaff. "We should start making up some new stories and telling them to the seeds. Just imagine all the exciting books that might bloom!"

Weatherstaff nodded eagerly.

Just then there was a bright pink flash and Trixi appeared, spinning round in the air on her leaf.

"Trixi!" cried Ellie. "Did you...?"

"I did!" Trixi
cried in delight.
"I gave the
book bud
to Aunt
Maybelle.
She was
really
pleased.
We only
need
one more
ingredient now!"

The sprites
overheard. "You picked a book bud?"
one of them demanded.

Trixi and the girls nodded. "They
appeared when we were telling the
story," Ellie admitted.

Jasmine put her hands on her hips. "And there's not much you can do about it now, is there?"

The sprite looked at her and then his shoulders sagged. "I suppose there isn't," he admitted. "And actually... well..." He looked down and seemed almost embarrassed. "It was worth it to hear such a good story! Thank you," he muttered.

Summer blinked in astonishment.

"Come on, let's go," he said hastily to the other sprites.

Summer watched them flapping slowly towards the door and felt her heart soften. Maybe the sprites weren't that bad after all!

But Dickon had gone over to the shelf where they had been standing. "Hey!" he sharply. "You've got some of our books!"

He was right! The sprites all had books hidden under their wings!

"It's not fair!" one of the sprites complained. "Why should you have all the books?"

"This is a library," Dickon explained. "You can borrow any of the books you want – but you have to ask us first and promise to bring them back."

Looking happy, the Storm Sprites flapped off.

Summer, Jasmine and Ellie chuckled. "I never imagined that the Storm Sprites would love reading so much," said Summer.

"Well, it's all because of you!" Dickon said.

"Your story *was* really good, girls!" said Trixi. "Can you tell me the end, please?"

They quickly finished it off for her.

"Oh, that's completely fluttery!" Trixi said, pirouetting in delight. "I'd love to read another story like that!"

"I'm going to speak to all the other brownies and get them telling lots of exciting stories to the trees and seeds straight away," said Dickon. "You know, we've always wondered why some buds grow faster than others. After what's happened today, I think it must be that the more exciting the story is, the faster the buds grow."

"From now on we'll tell lots of wonderful things to the trees and have more books – and more exciting stories – than ever!" said Weatherstaff. He frowned as a thought struck him. "Though...um...how are we going to think of the stories to tell?"

Dickon looked worried. "Yes, that is a problem."

Summer grinned at the others. "No,

it's not! I bet we can give you lots of ideas! Tell the trees stories where people rescue animals or go to faraway places and have magical adventures," she said, looking round at them all. "You could make up stories about flying carpets or genies in lamps or strange creatures."

The brownies started to whisper in surprise. "Genies? Flying carpets? Strange creatures?"

"Oh, I'd love to read stories like that!" said Trixi.

"Or you could tell them funny stories, like when wishes go wrong and crazy things happen or people live in strange lands like Upside Down Land," suggested Ellie.

"Or make up stories about acting and singing, about putting on shows and learning to dance," Jasmine put in eagerly. "You could tell stories about someone becoming a famous actress or singer or people travelling all over the place and performing in front of huge audiences."

"There are so many stories to tell!" Summer said to the book brownies. "We've given you some ideas just now but I bet you can think of lots more."

"All you have to do is use your imaginations," Ellie added.

"And most of all, tell stories you would like to read!" said Jasmine.

"Go and try, my friends!" Dickon urged. "Tell the trees the most exciting stories you can!"

The book brownies cheered and dashed off to the trees. They sat down around the trunks and started telling stories. After a few minutes green buds started popping out all over the branches.

"It's working!" cried Jasmine in delight.

Summer sighed happily. "It looks like Fairytale Forest is going to be just fine."

"Better than ever," said Ellie with a grin.

"And we only need one more ingredient for the counter-potion now," Summer pointed out.

"Which is lucky," said Trixi, sounding suddenly worried. "It's the Summer Ball in just two weeks! We must finish the potion before then or King Merry will be a stink toad forever!" She flew in circles around the girls' heads on her leaf.

"I think it's time for you to go back home now, but I'll send you another message very, very soon."

"We'll be looking out for it," Jasmine promised.

"Thank you!" Dickon called to the girls. "Thank you so much." All the other book brownies shouted thank you as well.

"See you again one day, I hope!" Summer said, waving to them.

Then the three girls held hands and
Trixi tapped her ring. A cloud of silver
sparkles surrounded them and whisked
them away. When the whirlwind
stopped they landed with a bump back
in Honeyvale Library, beside the dusty
old journals. The Magic Box was on the
floor in front of them.

"We're back!" said Summer as the sparkles faded.

Ellie scooped the Magic Box up and put it back in her bag. "What an amazing adventure!"

"And now we've only got one more ingredient to find!" said Jasmine.

Summer looked anxious. "Queen Malice is going to be furious when she finds out!"

"Good," said Jasmine. "She'll be even more mad when we get the last ingredient!" She jumped to her feet. "Now, I'm going to go and borrow that Pandora Parks book – I have to find out what happens next."

Ellie chuckled and got to her feet too. "I bet it won't be as good as the story we just made up!"

"Or as exciting as the adventure we just had," put in Summer.

"Not even the best book in the world could be as exciting as actually *going* to the Secret Kingdom," Jasmine said.

Even Summer had to agree with her. "I wonder when we can go back and find the last ingredient," she said longingly.

"Well, whenever it is, we'll be ready," said Ellie. "We're going to save King Merry from turning into a stink toad and nothing's going to stop us!"

The three girls looked at each other.
"Nothing at all!" they declared.

In the next Secret Kingdom adventure, Ellie, Summer and Jasmine visit

Midnight Maze

Read on for a sneak peek...

Summer Fun

The smell of burgers cooking on the barbecue drifted across the Honeyvale School playground. Adults and children wandered around brightly coloured stalls – the lucky dip, the cake stall and the bouncy castle. Sitting behind the face-painting table, Summer Hammond put down her book and sighed happily. She loved the school fete.

Beside her, her friend Ellie finished painting a tiger face onto Finn, Summer's little brother. "What do you think?" she asked, holding up a mirror.

Finn roared. "I'm the best tiger ever!"

"I've got a tiger joke for you, Finn," Ellie said. "Which day do tigers eat the most people?"

"I don't know! Which day?" asked Finn curiously.

"*Chews*-day!" Ellie grinned.

Finn giggled. Summer shook her head as she laughed. Ellie was always telling jokes, and some of them were really bad!

"I'm going to have another go at the lucky dip. Thanks, Ellie." Finn jumped up and ran away.

"I love face-painting!" Ellie said

happily, pushing her red curls back behind her ears.

"You're brilliant at it." Summer had been reading a fairy tale book while Ellie painted the faces. Now she started to tidy away the brushes. It had been really busy when they first started but the queue had finally quietened down. She checked her watch. "Olivia and Maddie should be coming to swap over with us soon, then we can go and look round the fete ourselves."

"And find Jasmine. I wonder how she's been getting on?" Ellie thought out loud.

Jasmine was their other best friend. She had decided to dress up as a wise woman and tell people's fortunes.

"We'll have to drag her away from fortune-telling for a while," said

Summer. "I want to buy some fairy cakes from the cake stall. They look yummy."

"Not as yummy as *real* fairy cakes," said Ellie.

They smiled at each other.

"Definitely not!" said Summer. She grinned as she thought about the amazing secret she shared with her two best friends. They had a magic box that could whisk them away to an enchanted land called the Secret Kingdom. The box had been made by King Merry, the kindly ruler there. When the beautiful kingdom had been in trouble, the box had come into the human world to find the only people that could help – Summer, Ellie and Jasmine!

"Do you remember when we ate fairy

cakes that turned us into fairies for a few minutes?" Summer whispered.

Ellie nodded. "And those flying cupcakes we saw at Sugarsweet Bakery that really flew in the air."

Summer sighed longingly. "Oh, I hope Trixi sends us a message in the Magic Box soon. We must go back – King Merry still needs our help."

The king's wicked sister, Queen Malice, caused all sorts of problems in the Secret Kingdom. Her most recent evil plan had been to trick King Merry into eating a cursed marshmallow cake, and now the king was slowing turning into a horrible creature called a stink toad. Only a counter-potion made from six rare ingredients could break the spell. Ellie, Summer and Jasmine had found five of the ingredients so far, but time was running out. If King Merry didn't drink the counter-potion by midnight on the night of the Summer Ball, he would be a stink toad for ever.

"King Merry was acting really like a toad when we saw him last," Ellie said anxiously. "I hope he hasn't got any worse."

Summer nodded. She loved the jolly, round king and she hated the thought of him turning into a stink toad. Luckily he didn't realise what was happening because his royal pixie, Trixi, and her wise aunt, Maybelle, had cast a spell to make everyone forget all about the curse, so that no one panicked while Summer, Ellie and Jasmine were busy finding the ingredients for the counter-potion.

"I wonder what the last ingredient will be," said Summer.

Just then, Olivia and Maddie came to take over the face-painting stall and Summer and Ellie quickly stopped talking.

"Thanks for taking over," Ellie said to the other girls.

Summer pushed her book into her pocket as she and Ellie hurried to find Jasmine's stall. It was a stripy tent with a large notice in swirly letters outside:

Madame Jasmina Rose. Fortune Teller Extraordinaire.

Come inside. If you dare…

As they reached the tent, a Year Three girl came out. "Oh, wow," she said, looking dazed. "I've got to remember my lucky number is eight so I can have lots of good luck from now on!"

Ellie and Summer giggled and poked their heads into the tent. Jasmine was sitting behind a table. She was wearing a long, colourful skirt and shawl and had a scarf tied round her head, over her long dark hair. She grinned when she saw them. "Ah, two pretty little girls," she said in a quavering voice, just like an old woman. "Come to hear your fortunes, have you, my sweeties?" Clutching her shawl around herself, she beckoned to them, her dark eyes teasing.

Read

Midnight Maze

to find out what happens next!

Secret Kingdom

Be in on the secret.
Collect them all!

Series 1

When Jasmine, Summer and Ellie discover
the magical land of the Secret Kingdom,
a whole world of adventure awaits!

Secret Kingdom

Bubble
Volcano

ROSIE BANKS

Dream Dale

ROSIE BANKS

Sugarsweet
Bakery

ROSIE BANKS

Lily Pad
Lake

ROSIE BANKS

Midnight
Maze

ROSIE BANKS

Fairytale
Forest

ROSIE BANKS

Series 2

Wicked Queen Malice has cast a spell to
turn King Merry into a toad! Can the girls
find six magic ingredients to save him?

Secret Kingdom

Series 3

When Queen Malice releases six fairytale
baddies into the Secret Kingdom, it's up to the
girls to find them!

Have you read all the books in Series Four?

Meet the magical Animal Keepers of the
Secret Kingdom, who spread fun, friendship,
kindness and bravery throughout the land!

Secret Kingdom

A magical world of
friendship and fun!

Join the Secret Kingdom Club at

www.secretkingdombooks.com

and enjoy games, sneak peeks and lots more!

You'll find great activities, competitions, stories
and games, plus a special newsletter for
Secret Kingdom friends!